Tom in the Middle

by Berthe Amoss

Harper & Row, Publishers

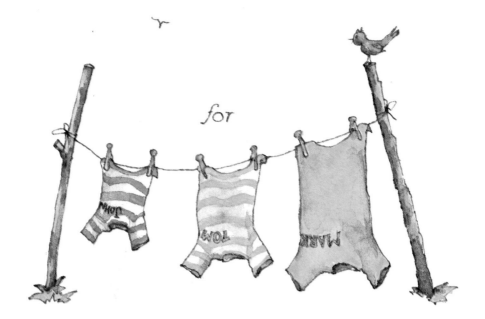

for

Tom in the Middle
Copyright © 1968, 1988 by Berthe Amoss
All rights reserved. No part of this book may be
used or reproduced in any manner whatsoever without
written permission except in the case of brief quotations
embodied in critical articles and reviews. Printed in
the United States of America. For information address
Harper & Row Junior Books, 10 East 53rd Street,
New York, N.Y. 10022. Published simultaneously in
Canada by Fitzhenry & Whiteside Limited, Toronto.

10 9 8 7 6 5 4 3 2 1

Revised Edition, newly illustrated

Library of Congress Cataloging-in-Publication Data
Amoss, Berthe.
    Tom in the middle.

    Summary: Tom has a little brother who follows him
everywhere and hurts his toys and books, and an older
brother who can do almost everything and won't let Tom
play with his things.
    [1. Brothers—Fiction]   I. Title.
PZ7.A5177To 1988   [Fic]   86-42991
ISBN 0-06-020063-4
ISBN 0-06-020064-2 (lib. bdg.)

Tom in the Middle

I have a little brother named John.

He's so little he doesn't talk yet,
except he knows my name.
"Tom," he says, and then he follows me.

5

He follows me *everywhere.*

If I ride my bike, he wants to ride with me.

When I spin round, he spins round

and makes me konk my head.

When I swing, he stands in the way.

"*Move*," I say, and he smiles. He stands there.

Mother says, "Don't swing so high, dear.

You might hit John."

9

If I build a house with blocks,
he knocks it down.
One time I let him be Hurricane Betsy,
but he can't be Hurricane Betsy every time.

10

Not if I build a good house.

John loses parts of my game.
"Plunk," he says. "Plunk, plunk."

Yesterday he tore my book. My favorite book.
Mother said, "Tom, John didn't tear your book
on purpose. It was an accident. You shouldn't
have hit him. He's so little."

He's so little I quit playing with him.
I have a big brother to play with.
His name is Mark. He's bigger than I am
and *much* bigger than John.

Mark can do almost everything.

He reads books without pictures,
and he goes to school by himself.

Sometimes he lets me carry his lunch box.

Sometimes we fight. Last night in the tub
Mark said, "Give me the soap, stupid."
I said, "Stupid yourself,"
and threw the soap on the floor.
Mother said, "*Out,* both of you,
and *no* bubble bath tonight!"

Mark can play Monopoly.

Yesterday, when Mark was in school,

I played Monopoly by myself.

When Mark came home, he said,

"Who's been playing with my Monopoly?"

"Tom," John said.

"You've got all the $100 bills

mixed up with the $500's," Mark said.

"DON'T PLAY WITH MY THINGS ANYMORE!"

I'm going to hide from Mark and John.

I'm going to put on my policeman suit,

and I'm going to hide in my secret place,
and when John calls, "Tom!"
I won't even answer.

And when Mark calls, "Tommy!"
I'll pretend I don't hear.
Then I can be by myself all day long.

23

And when night comes—

when night comes—

when night comes,

I'll go inside.

It's warmer there.

John and I will eat bread and butter with sugar.

Then we'll make a tent with John's blue blanket

and be sleeping Indians.

And Mark can stand watch for us.